susan vinson

Published in Australia by …

First published in Australia 2019
This edition published 2019
Copyright © Susan Vinson 2018
Cover design, typesetting: WorkingType (www.workingtype.com.au)

Susan Vinson
Jet Black
ISBN: 978 - 0 - 646 - 80964 - 9
pp130

Susan has been an avid reader all her life. English History, the natural world and ancient myths having been of special interest to her.

She grew up in the western suburbs of Sydney, and has travelled extensively around Australia. She is a trained beauty therapy and has practiced and taught Yoga for many years.

Susan has a keen interest in all kinds of art and antiques, especially mosaics.

She has two wonderful adult children and *Jet Black* is her fourth book.

Author's Note

This is a dark fantasy story about a mysterious necklace, made in the Celtic times of England by a gifted craftsman for his queen. This Celtic clan also revered a warrior goddess called 'The Morrigan' and carved on the necklace is one of her earthly forms, a raven. But the necklace has also been imbued with a mystical power, awakened by blood, to summon this goddess.

The Morrigan represents a very powerful female deity of war, death and prophecy. She can take on many other forms, from a beautiful woman to an old hag to another animal. The necklace travels through time, through many countries and many families, carrying with it the power of the mighty and mysterious Morrigan.

The main characters of the story are all woman, who, although living hundreds of years apart, faced the same dilemmas, dangers and struggles. I have endeavoured to weave a mythical thread through the story of how the necklace carries the power of the Goddess within it.

This is my fourth book and I hope you find it interesting and thought-provoking.

Thank you for reading.

Susan Vinson

*Ravens have long been associated
with prophecy and death*

Britain, In the Time of the Romans

ltwidus found it hard to focus. His eyes were weary after nights working by the firelight, but he knew time was running out — his life was waning. The joints of his fingers were stiff and swollen, and his hands were no longer steady. His back ached but he worked feverishly to finish the piece, something that would be a fitting tribute to his goddess before he died ... he would never worship the Roman gods covering his lands. The hatred for these brutal invaders, who had killed so many of his tribe, ran deep in his veins, burning his soul.

The black amber stone he bought from a trader was perfect; as Altwidus stared into its depths, he saw the soul of his true goddess reflected. She was a female warrior, old as time, sometimes called 'The Morrigan': a shape shifter, black as night. One of her favourite earthly forms was of a raven, and so this was the creature Altwidus carved so deftly into the smooth surface of the stone. It was framed in gold, carved with an intricate pattern of intertwining circles. The chain was strong, made from Welsh gold. The wearer would always feel its weight around their neck, feel its strength … and its protection.

Finally, the last feather was carved; Altwidus let a rare smile light up his weathered face. His grey eyes shone with joy and he felt a surge of energy run through his old body. The raven looked alive with its oily black feathers shining in the firelight; its eye looked back at him, as if perceiving his thoughts. He held the stone reverently, mesmerised by its beauty. Although it looked like black ice, it emanated the warmth of a living soul.

Altwidus wrapped the stone in a soft cloth and bound it carefully; he had used all his wealth to make it, and tomorrow he would present it to his clan's queen. Her name was Oifa. She was worthy of such a gift — it would give her strength with her war against the Roman invaders. They did not respect our women leaders, taking our land and disrespecting our gods. Altwidus spat on the floor in disgust. He was glad his life was ending, and he would not have to endure the Roman yoke for much longer.

The next day, Altwidus patiently waited to be presented to Oifa; she had many people to see. He washed himself that morning, a rare event for him, and he put on the his best clothes. His teeth were picked clean and his hair was combed. He hoped he looked presentable enough for such a fine woman.

When he was summoned into her presence, he bowed low and held the gift out for her, hoping she didn't notice his shaking hands. He slowly straightened himself and met her eyes; she smiled warmly and beckoned for him to come closer, his heartbeat faster as he stepped toward his leader.

Oifa sat regally, her arms resting on the ornately carved arms of her throne; she looked magnificent to him. Her dress was made of fine cloth, deep blue with gold trimmings; her long red hair was intricately plaited and held in place with haircombs made from bone with animals carved on them. The only jewellery she wore was a thick gold torque around her neck and a gold bracelet in the shape of a serpent with green stones for eyes; both pieces were expertly made and Altwidus suddenly felt his work would be inadequate.

'A gift, my queen — I hope it is worthy of you,' said Altwidus humbly.

Oifa took the gift, and when she unwrapped the cloth, her eyes lit up with joy at the stone's beauty. The bird almost looked alive, and she knew it represented The Morrigan. The goddess of battle and death, the scald crow; she can be seen as a beautiful woman or a terrifying old hag. Sometimes she would take the form of a wolf, an eel or a cow; she can appear in the air, on land, and in the water… she has many powers and skills.

'You are truly a magician, Altwidus, to create such a piece; I will treasure it for the rest of my life. I hope I am worthy of the goddess and I accept this gift with gratitude. I invite you to feast with my family today to show my appreciation.'

'Thank you, my queen,' Altwidus blushed at the praise and bowed low before taking his leave.

Oifa removed the gold torque from around her neck and placed it reverently beside her chair. She rarely took it off, but this necklace was enchant-ing and she had to wear it. Carefully she lifted it around her neck — she could feel its weight, and admired its beauty. She touched the raven, tracing the intricate detail with her fingertips, and then clasped it, letting its warmth flow into her fingers. She would wear it always, even in death.

Oifa died in battle six months later. The Roman army had surrounded her warriors — who, although brave, could not withstand the disciplined onslaught of the Roman soldiers. Their strong shields and short stabbing swords cut her people to pieces; it was a horrible sight and it spurred Oifa to fight on until the end.

The Romans found it shocking that these barbarians allowed their women to fight; it was another reason to think that they were superior to these natives of Britain.

The raven necklace swung about Oifa's neck as she battled on. She was proud to have killed many Roman soldiers before she received a fatal stab wound. As she lay dying, her blood seeped into the black stone, awakening its power. As she lost consciousness, she heard the cry of the raven, and she knew her goddess had come for her, proud she died in battle. With her last breath, Oifa's spirit joined the large black bird that hovered above her, and then it disappeared into the sky.

Some of the Roman soldiers saw the mysterious

black shape which hovered over the pagan leader's body. Many of the soldiers would not mention what they saw, silently praying to their gods when the battle had finally ceased, then cursing these pagan lands and its people. But they did allow their enemies to bury their queen with due ceremony.

Oifa was buried with great respect, her body washed clean of blood and dirt and laid out on a gold chariot. She was dressed in her finest clothes; the soft shoes that clad her feet had gold thread on them. A splendid torque with horse heads encircled her neck, and she had glass bead bracelets on her wrists. Her hands were folded on her chest, clasping the black raven necklace. Her battle weapons were placed beside her; the sword was bronze and enamel with an ornately carved bone handle, and a long spear and a quiver of arrows would always be within her reach. Pots of food and drink were also left for her comfort in the other world, known as The Fortress of Shadows.

*　*　*

Over the centuries, many of these Celtic graves were plundered and the riches stolen. Oifa's necklace was traded east to Byzantium, then back west to Budapest, then to St Petersburg, then to Paris. Nonbelievers protected it through the centuries; they understood its worth and power. The old beliefs were trampled over by the conquerors, then superseded by those who thought their gods superior.

But the goddess never went away. She was always there, and you only needed to believe in her, summon her.

*   *   *

Altwidus closed his home and workshop the day after feasting with his queen, and travelled into the woods, carrying a little food and a blanket. He built a fire and made offerings of jet, this wondrous black stone, to his goddess and asked for her blessing. He spent one night in the woods, listening to the sounds of the creatures that came to life in the darkness. He went to sleep to the mournful sound of an owl in the distance; it gave him comfort, reminding him he wasn't alone. He had many dreams that night; in one of them he saw Oifa die, her spirit carried away by a raven to the otherworld. He didn't feel the tears that fell from the corners of his eyes as he slept; his heart had always belonged to his queen.

He never woke from his sleep, and soon a dark shape wearing a long cloak hovered nearby, eventually taking the form of a woman. She was tall and had long black hair which hid her face; her bare feet trod lightly on the forest floor as she moved silently towards his body. Her eyes were hooded, but fierce and unwavering as she surveyed her surroundings. The animals of the forest gathered, quietly paying homage to this great queen spirit. She saw the offerings made by Altwidus and was pleased at this mortal's respect for her.

Then she became a maelstrom of black feathers, changing her shape back into a raven, and took Altwidus's soul to the other world, which was called Tír na nÓg.

She is blood and battle and death

The blade that cleaves flesh from the bone

That cuts the old from the new

That reshapes, remakes, redefines us

Blood is not to be feared; it is the current of life

Battle is not to be feared; it is the price of sovereignty

Death is not to be feared; it is the end of the old …

And a new beginning, endlessly

(Poem for The Morrigan, Morgan Daimler)

France,
1722

It was hard for Margarite to keep her eyes open. The party wasn't that entertaining and she was tired of listening to her travelling companion snoring and gasping in the corner of the carriage. She looked across at him, slouched with his mouth open; his cravat was stained with wine and food, and his breeches strained to hold his fat belly in check.

Margarite turned away in disgust, wishing she was asleep in her bed. She played with her necklace as she stared out into the darkness — this strange necklace, which her husband had bought at an auction. He didn't like it particularly, but he knew it was worth a great deal. The countess loved it the moment she saw it. Others at the party commented on it and the countess felt different when she wore it … more confident, even powerful.

Her thoughts were interrupted by shouting, and the carriage lurched to an abrupt halt; the horses stamped their feet and shook their heads, making their bridles jingle loudly. The driver struggled to calm them. She guessed they were being robbed, but it didn't worry her too much, as they'd only want their valuables.

The marquis was thrown forward and hit his head. Waking up in pain, he started to stick his head out to curse the driver. His demeanour changed when he saw the robbers and their pistols pointed at him. He looked across at the countess; his face was pale, his body tense, locked in fear. 'We are being robbed, oh my lord, how dare they! Just keep calm Madame, I will protect you!'

'Thank you Phillipe, I trust in your bravery,' Margarite said insincerely as she peered out into the darkness, trying to see what the robbers looked like. Suddenly, the night seemed more exciting.

There were three of them, their faces covered, but only one of them spoke. His accent was foreign, but he spoke with authority and appeared calm and in control. Phillipe stiffened and sat upright, puffing his chest out; the buttons on his britches strained to hold his huge girth. One of the robbers peered into the carriage and looked from one passenger to the other. Margarite pulled her velvet cape tightly around her to hide the necklace, which was the one thing she didn't want to give up.

'Get out, kind sir, if you please … and hand over your valuables,' said the robber, feigning courtesy.

The marquis obliged, mumbling his outrage as he struggled outside. 'Do you know who I am? I'll have you hanged, you thief.'

'Just hand over everything of value and I'll spare your life,' said the masked man quietly.

The marquis handed over his belongings to one

of the other robbers, who then roughly pushed the marquis onto the muddy ground. He fell face down, swallowing some of the muck which he spat out with outrage. His clothes were ruined. A gun was held to the back of his head while their leader moved his horse around to the other side of the carriage. He leant down to the countess, who was now a little frightened, but his dark eyes sparkled. Some of his curly hair broke free from their tie and fell wildly around his face, and his skin crinkled around his eyes — she knew he was smiling beneath his mask. 'Don't worry Madame, no one will be hurt if you hand over your jewels.' His tone was friendly and courteous.

'Thank you sir,' she said confidently, smiling and taking her time as she removed her jewellery, except for the raven necklace which she hoped had skipped his attention. The countess leaned out and dropped it all into the pouch he held open.

'Open your cape Madame,' said the leader, gesturing with his pistol.

'Please, oh really sir … for a minute there I thought you were a gentleman.'

'I can assure you Madame, I am, but I want the necklace as well,' he said quietly.

'But it's very special to me, the other pieces are worth more,' pleaded the countess.

The robber held out his hand patiently, so she took it off and dropped it into his hands grudgingly. He looked at the necklace; even in the dark, the stone glowed with strange warmth, and the raven's eye seemed real. He could feel the weight of the gold and he knew it was worth a great deal. He smiled to himself … this will be for Sofia.

'Thank you Madame.'

The robber tipped his hat and signalled his men, and they all rode away at high speed, disappearing into the night.

Margarite felt cheated that she had lost the necklace, but also exhilarated with that bit of excitement, and no physical harm was done. She had laughed to herself when the marquis was made to lay face down in the mud; he would be so outraged to be shamed like that. He started to tidy himself up with the help of the driver, whom he eventually snapped at and pushed away, telling him to get a move on towards the count's manor. But she had to act appropriately, so Margarite quickly feigned concern when he was back in the carriage, and praised his actions. He railed against the robbers all the way home as he kept trying to clean the muck off his face and clothes. Margarite listened patiently and offered her kerchief, but smiled secretly in the darkness as she thought about the mystery thief.

Her husband was outraged; Margarite soon excused herself, saying she was exhausted and needed to sleep. The marquis was invited to stay the night and she left the room with him retelling the details of the robbery to her husband Louis.

'He was just a common thief; the authorities will get him and he'll hang one day, like they all do. But be assured, your lordship, that I would have given my life to protect the countess.'

'Thank you Phillipe, I'm glad you could be of

service.' The count turned away, doubting the man's ability to do anything.

'I'll call for a servant to assist you to wash, and I'll have some clean attire for you to change into. I bid you a good night's rest sir.' The count smiled and left the room, glad to be rid of the man.

'Oh yes, indeed it has been a long night. Thank you, dear sir.' The marquis helped himself to another glass of wine to calm his nerves.

The only thing Margarite regretted was the loss of the raven necklace; she only had it for a year but she had grown attached to it. There was something about it; when she wore it, she felt a power she couldn't explain, and it wasn't like any other piece of jewellery she had ever owned.

When she finally was resting in her bed, she found it hard to sleep, tossing and turning, her mind going over the events of the night and what story she would give to the authorities … she hoped the robber wasn't caught. Looking into his eyes made her heart beat a little faster, something she hadn't felt in many years.

The marquis made himself the hero of the night and her husband vowed to hunt down the culprit, while buying more jewellery to replace what had been stolen.

The countess gave few details to the lawmen about the robbery, saying it was too dark and she was too distressed to notice much. But she told a different story to her friends, and the young men hung off her every word at all the glittering occasions that year. It was a story of a daring robber, with mischievous eyes and charming manners, and a mysterious necklace which he stole for his lover.

South Coast of England, 1723

Sofia's heart skipped a beat when she glimpsed *The Sea Witch* through the trees, sitting calmly in the bay. It was a beautiful ship with its carved figurehead of a woman with wild eyes and long dark hair looking out from her prow, her scarlet dress barely covering her shapely bosom and the hem falling around her tiny bare feet. Her palms were open to the sea as if to welcome the waves that would break against the bow as long as she sailed. The ship's impossibly tall masts, ropes and sails being tended by the men, the huge anchor chain disappearing into the water — it was a world far removed from her own … and it was his world.

She'd met him by chance in the town market, as he was running from a constable. Sofia recognised the lawman; he was on her husband's payroll and a thug. It would be satisfying to thwart her husband in some way, so when the outlaw tripped and fell near her, ripping his stocking and cursing, Sofia decided she would help him.

When he looked up and saw her, his face broke into a smile, and he started apologising for his language. Sofia was dumbstruck; he was the most handsome man she had ever seen, but the constable was closing in and shouting loudly so there was no time for talk. He jumped up, looking worried now, so Sofia beckoned for him to follow her down a side street, hiding him under a fruit barrow which she stood in front of, pretending to buy some fruit. Her wide skirts hid him from view, and Sofia blushed suddenly, thinking of him down there so close.

When the coast was clear he jumped up, introducing himself as Raimondo and thanking her with a kiss — Sofia didn't have time to protest. 'I have to go. Meet me here next Wednesday, same time, I'll wait for you … goodbye and thank you,' he quickly said before bowing and disappearing into the back streets.

Sofia was speechless and stood for a while, trying to regain her composure. She wandered home in a daze, thinking of that kiss. And from that day on, he became her one joy in her unhappy marriage, and he became everything to her.

But this day was the last time she would see her lover; he had to leave England again because he was in great danger now. Sofia patiently waited in the cottage for Raimondo, but she was growing anxious and started to wring her hands constantly. She was worried someone would discover them and pounce; Raimondo and his men had accomplished many successful robberies but the nobility would no longer allow such losses without punishment. If she were caught, she would probably go to gaol, but she didn't care anymore. His fate would be far worse … hanging.

They would only have a few hours at best, and when he silently appeared, as he always seemed to do, she felt that the world stood still when their eyes met. They embraced each other tightly and loved one another like there was no tomorrow, but the time seemed to go so fast and their hearts slowly filled with the pain of their coming final goodbye.

They quietly held hands as they walked back to the beach — no words were needed. Then they embraced tightly, never wanting to let go. They stayed close, Sofia with her head against his chest as Raimondo gently stroked her dark hair. They silently watched the anchor being raised and the sails hauled up, catching the breeze and making the ship come to life.

Before he let her go, he lifted the necklace and held the stone in his hands; it slowly warmed his fingers. He put it against his chest and held it there. He closed his eyes and made a silent wish to the raven, truly believing with all his soul that it would come true one day.

Gently, Raimondo pushed Sofia away; he gripped her shoulders and stared hard into her face. 'We will meet again, my love, one day. I know it. I will never forget you.'

He kissed her hands one more time and Sofia let her tears fall. She could not speak; she wanted to follow him and never let go, no matter the consequences. She watched his purposeful steps as he walked towards the rowboat waiting to take him to his ship; her eyes willed him to turn around, but he did not look back.

Sofia stood barefoot in the shallows, watching his ship disappear into the horizon. She knew he stood on the deck, watching her, until he could see her no more. She clutched the necklace he had given her; it felt cold at first but soon it warmed her fingers. It looked like a piece of black ice. Every detail of the engraved bird was captured; you almost believed it could take flight. Sofia wished she could fly now and go to her love, but she was a mere mortal destined to live out her fate with her feet firmly on the ground. It was the most beautiful gift she had ever received in her life. Sofia knew he stole it, but that's what pirates do; he gave it to her as a parting gift because they knew their 'goodbye' would be forever.

'Promise me you will wear it always, Sofia. Somehow I believe this necklace will protect you and return you to me one day. Promise … it will give me hope to know you're wearing it, my love.'

Sofia had laughed at first when he said these words, him being an outlaw and all, but when she saw the earnest look on his face she realised how much it meant to him. 'I promise, my love. It's so beautiful, thank you — I'll never take it off,' said Sofia, wanting to reassure him.

Sofia had touched his face one last time before Raimondo turned and strode away without looking back; it was the only way he could keep himself from staying and endangering them both.

France was his best chance of escape, because

he knew people there he trusted and who could hide him. She concentrated her thoughts, wanting to remember everything about him; they had such a short time together, but it would have to last a lifetime. All she really knew about him was that his mother was Corsican and his father died when he was young, and that she loved him with all her heart. But she was a married woman and he an outlaw, so it could never be, no matter how much they loved each other.

The sun was setting, changing the colour of the ocean to a deep blue, its dying rays casting a golden glow across the horizon. She stood, searching the expanse of the ocean, even though the ship was no longer in view. But she could not bring herself to leave; she wanted this moment to last forever, and keep at bay the crushing loneliness that was filling her soul.

Raimondo stood tall, his gaze never leaving the tiny shape of Sofia clad in her red cape, standing on the shore. He wanted to remember every moment of their goodbye, the passion of her kiss, the softness of her skin and the intensity of her gaze. She had the most beautiful eyes he had ever seen, the colour of amethyst — so different to his own, that were as black as night. They both knew they would never see each other again in this life, so Raimondo drank in her image like a man dying of thirst. She was the only woman he had ever loved beside his spirited mother; he was sure she would have loved Sofia if they had ever met.

The ocean grew turbulent, roughly tossing the boat as they left the bay and reached the open ocean. Raimondo knew the men needed his guidance now; he had to let go of his vigil. With a heavy heart, he turned away and looked to the darkening sky. He was sure her husband had not discovered their love and she would be safe, albeit unhappy with him. He wished he had the power to save her from her life, but he didn't, and the law would only be satisfied when he was hanging at the end of a rope. The wind blew stronger now, whipping the sea spray into Raimondo's face; its sting broke his reverie and he shouted his orders in a voice which told the crew he was back in charge.

Raimondo's heartache was short lived; he died a year later in a fight with the British Navy. He found himself surrounded and outgunned, dying in a sword fight. He had vowed long ago never to be taken prisoner — to spend time in some filthy gaol, then hanged. As he lay dying from his fatal wounds, his last thought was for the only person left in the world he loved … Sofia.

The British officers had the bodies of the dead pirates unceremoniously tossed into the sea; their flesh would be devoured by predators, but their spirits would now abide in the wild ocean, untamed by man, untamed by man, where Manann, the son of the ocean, dwells …

Edward, the coach driver, doffed his cap and approached Sofia hesitantly. 'We must leave now, my lady — we have a long journey and it's getting late.'

'Yes, I'm coming,' said Sofia absentmindedly.

Sofia sat in the coach, staring out at the growing darkness, feeling numb. When they finally entered the gates of the manor, Sofia's stomach churned. Her husband Maximillian would be waiting; his anger would be brewing away in his evil, jealous mind. His fits of temper were getting worse along with his drunkenness, and Sofia knew he had discovered her secret; he had pretended for a while, playing cat and mouse with her, but his vindictiveness would soon break through.

Sofia had tried to love her husband at first, but she hated him now. Max knew Sofia did not love him. Not that he cared particularly; she was just another thing he owned and there were women everywhere eager to sleep with him. They were both bound by a marriage of the church, and they could only be parted by death. Loving Raimondo was the only joy in Sofia's life and it gave her strength to endure her lot with her husband … but what would she have to cling to now?

Maximillian's first wife died suddenly; no children had come from their union, and so it wasn't long before he was looking to marry again. Sofia's father had done some carpentry work for Lord Rains, and he had seen Sofia when he came to inspect his order. Sofia hadn't noticed him watching her as she did her chores and had never spoken to him; unbeknown to Sofia, he had approached her father enquiring about her age and education. It was not long before Sofia was presented to him and he started sending her gifts; her family convinced her of her luck to marry someone of his status, and the marriage was arranged.

His demeanour changed once the ring was on her finger, from a charming nobleman to a fearful, controlling brute. Every day, he reminded her of her lowly background. Sofia grew to avoid him when possible, especially when he had been drinking. She was also aware of the other women he frequently visited; it was a relief for her when his attentions were elsewhere, so she would not have to accept his advances. And Sofia no longer cared who laughed behind her back at the many social functions they attended; she realised very quickly that she would never be accepted in this new society, full of high-born people.

The carriage pulled up and Edward opened the door for her. She briefly caught a glimpse of the pity in his eyes as he looked at her, but he quickly dropped his gaze and offered his hand. Sofia took it, and thanked him as she stepped out into the darkness. Her tiny feet hardly made a sound on the gravel as she walked towards the house. The night air was cold, so she hugged her cape tightly around herself; it felt like her only protection now. She looked up at the only lit window in the house and saw the silhouette of her husband staring down at her. Sofia looked away quickly.

The butler stood ready with the door open for her. 'Good evening, my lady. Lord Rains requested you come to the library and he will be there shortly to greet you. The fire has been lit for your comfort,' said Tomlins as he bowed subserviently and let her pass.

'Thank you,' Sofia said as she hurried pass. She didn't trust him; he would do anything for Maximillian.

Sofia climbed the stairs, and with each step her fear grew; she tried to think of what she would say to him. She looked at the huge painting of Maximillian's father hanging before her at the top of the stairs; he had the same cold blue eyes and arrogant face. Sofia hated the painting. Finally reaching the library door, she paused, straightening her hair and dress. The door was slightly ajar. She slowly pushed the door and stepped timidly inside; it was dark except for the light of the fire. Sofia thought she was alone until she heard her husband speak.

'Good evening, my dear, I've been waiting for you. Was it a pleasant visit with your cousin?'

Sofia turned in the direction of the voice, and in an armchair sat Maximillian. Despite his polite address, she heard the cold edge in his voice.

'Oh … you startled me; I couldn't see you there sitting in the dark. Yes my dear, Camille is in fine spirits, and sends her greetings,' said Sofia as calmly as she could.

Maximillian quietly sat there, enjoying his

wife's discomfort; then he spoke, making Sofia jump. 'Why are you lying to me? You harlot, I know you were with him. I've heard he's a common thief, do you have no shame? They will catch him, you know, and maybe you along with him,' Maximillian shouted angrily as he slammed his fist into the desk. Sofia's mind was scrambling to find the right words to appease him, and then he stood up and lurched toward her.

'You've been drinking again; you're not thinking straight. I went to see Camille … come, why don't we have dinner and have a good night's rest?' Sofia said hopefully.

Sofia edged around the desk, trying to guess his movements and avoid his lunges, he tripped, cursing, getting angrier.

'I'll kill you, you're a whore, and the punishment for adultery is death. But I'm not waiting for the courts to do it.' Maximillian wore a maniacal grin now, and his eyes blazed with hatred — he craved violence. Sofia saw the glint of the knife he was carrying in the firelight, and she began to panic.

'Husband, I know you have other women ... and yes, I was with him and I love him, and I am not ashamed. Do you think adultery is a greater sin than murder?' Sofia said, raising her voice defiantly.

She desperately made a dash for the door, but instead she felt his grip wrap around her arm. She cried out in pain as he swung her around to face him, then plunged the knife deep into her chest. The last thing Sofia saw was the twisted expression on her husband's face, his lust for blood ... her blood. She clutched her chest, trying to plug the fatal wound. The pain was terrible at first, but she faded quickly and crumpled to the floor ... dead. Maximillian stood for a while, looking down upon his wife lying on the floor, the knife obscenely sticking out of her chest. Her face had turned a deathly white, her beautiful violet eyes staring wide open ... into oblivion.

Her blood spread rapidly from the wound, changing the colour of her dress from soft pink to a garish red. Sofia's bloody fingers held the black stone tightly and the blood seeped into its depths, awakening an ancient spirit which answered the voice of the dead.

The raven followed Sofia's soul as it left her mortal body and heard its dying wish, and promised that one day her wish would be fulfilled … one day, but she must wait until the time was right.

Max leant down and ripped the necklace away from around her neck, covering his hands in blood. He stared at it, thinking it might be worth something, so he cleaned it and put it in the drawer. He felt calmness descend upon him now, His anger had been satiated; he felt nothing for his wife. How dare she treat him like that, him a Lord, and she nothing but a commoner, which he had condescended to marry!

Tomlins helped his master get rid of his wife's body; he hid his shock at the sight of Sofia. He thought her a timid low-born girl, but she didn't deserve to die like this. However, he said nothing and did what he was told to do; he was in no position to question his master. He wrapped her body in a sheet and tied it off with ropes, and then they both went out into the darkness, careful no one was awake watching them do their dirty work. Lord Rains was having one of his gardens renovated on his large estate and they buried Sofia's body where the gardeners were planting trees. Lord Rains ordered Tomlins to oversee the gardeners the next day and make sure nobody suspected anything. Tomlins was well rewarded for his help and silence. Edward was sacked immediately; Maximillian knew he had feelings for his wife and couldn't be trusted to keep his suspicions to himself.

The tree planted over Sofia's body was a rowan tree. It grew strong and tall, becoming a place where ravens gathered. In ancient mythological belief, the rowan represents physical and spiritual nourishment, transformation and liberation, union and fertility. It was bad luck to fell a rowan tree and burning one was taboo.

❋　❋　❋

Lord Rains feigned grief and hurt as he spread the rumour of his wife's infidelity and escape with a pirate. It was the talk for months at the dinner parties he attended, and a lot of the ladies giggled behind their fans, thinking it a very romantic story. Lord Rains remarried within two years to another, much younger woman, and was never brought to justice for his crime. He sold the necklace for a tidy sum; it was an attractive piece and he knew it was given to his wife by the thief, her lover. Some trinket he stole for the little tramp — he probably told her it was made for a queen.

Maximillian had a disagreement with his wife Bethany and was in a foul mood; the beating he gave his wife had not abated his anger, so he decided to go for a ride and work off some of his aggression elsewhere. His new mare was an Arab, highly spirited and pretty with her white blaze and chestnut coat. The mare was flighty, so Maximillian whipped her into a gallop straight away, making her work up a lather.

The rowan tree grew tall and strong, and always

the ravens came, sitting and watching quietly. The gardeners frequently shooed them away; they could not understand why they always sat in that particular tree. They felt it was an evil omen. The ravens watched Lord Rains ride off and they decided to follow. They kept their distance on high at first, but they signalled to each other and dived downward toward the horse and rider.

The mare moved her head abruptly to one side — some birds had flown right at her face, making her shy away erratically and run even faster. Lord Rains saw the birds right at the last minute and flung one of his arms out at them; he lost his balance and fell awkwardly, but his foot was caught in the stirrup and he was being dragged along by the mare. He desperately tried to free his leg but couldn't; soon the back of his head was bleeding and one arm was broken, along with some ribs. He kept struggling and was finally free of the stirrup when his ankle broke; he screamed out in pain, and then he lost consciousness.

He woke up disorientated and in agony. The

mare was gone and he wasn't sure how long he had been lying there.

He looked up at the cloudy sky, trying to guess the time, and convinced himself that someone would soon come looking for him. He tried to stand up but the pain was terrible and it was hard to breathe, so he just lay there staring up at the sky. A cool breeze made him shiver. He slowly looked around at his surroundings, trying to remember how far he had ridden from the house, but he couldn't concentrate and his mind went back to the pain. 'Those ravens … why did they fly at the horse like that? When I get back I'm going to shoot the lot of them. I'll have that tree where they sit burned down!'

As he lay there stricken, the ravens silently gathered around him. Maximillian saw them and started cursing at them, but when one jumped on his chest, staring at him with its cold black eye, he felt a shiver go up his spine. He had never felt so vulnerable, and when more of them moved closer, terror gripped his mind. He lifted his good arm when a raven went for his eye, trying to protect himself, but there were so many of them and he was so weak now. But he wasn't giving in yet.

He writhed and fought as best he could, punching and hitting with his one good arm. But the pain was taking over. Their long sharp beaks ripped and tore his skin to ribbons; it hung and flapped around him as he struggled, but the worst thing was the shock and agony of having his eyes ripped from their sockets. He screamed when he felt the last sinew being ripped away, and the odd emptiness he felt in his face where his eyeballs once sat. The ravens flung the severed eyes away; they now lay cold, hard and bloodied, staring at nothing. Now he realised the horror of dying ... defenceless, blind and alone. His body was a seething mass of black feathers, beaks and claws — and underneath his blood ran freely, staining the ground around him. Finally he lay still. He was no longer recognisable as Lord Maximillian Rains; he was now just a bloodied heap of flesh.

The ravens' work was done, one by one they

hopped down away from the body. They stayed to clean the flesh from their claws and preen their feathers. And as darkness fell, they took flight and disappeared silently into the night.

✳   ✳   ✳

Max's wife was glad to see him ride off and did not miss him, so it was many hours before the alarm was raised. The men had only a couple of hours of sunlight left, so they were relieved when they spotted the mare. She was standing quietly, eating the grass, her bridle dangling; then they found his body, not far away. It was cold and stiff by the time he was found. They couldn't believe what they saw; the bloody injuries he had sustained were not from a riding fall. The thing that shocked the men most was that his eyes had been pecked out.

They crossed themselves at the sight; it surely was the devil's work for a man to be attacked by birds like that. They knew their master wasn't a kind man and most of them were frightened of him, but still … to die like that? They all made a promise to try to keep this knowledge away from his wife. They were loath to touch his body at first, but they had to bring him back so they wrapped his body as best they could, especially his face, tied it to his mare and led her back. They all had trouble sleeping that night; the image of Lord Rains's face haunted their dreams.

Bethany was sitting in her room, thinking how much she hated Maximillian, when her maid delivered the news about his riding accident and death. Most of the grisly details were kept from her — for now, at least.

'Please Anna, leave me alone for a while. I do not want to be disturbed. Thank you.'

'Yes my lady.' Anna quietly closed the door, hoping Lady Rains would be alright.

Bethany sat down on the edge of her bed, staring into space, knowing her prayers had been answered.

The next day she had to identify her husband, and was escorted by her brother, Peter.

'I have to warn you, sister, your husband's body

is in a terrible state. 'His eyes have been removed … it must have been ravens, there are so many of them around,' said Peter, waiting for his sister's reaction, but she just stood quietly.

'Ravens, you say … we always see them in the garden, in the rowan tree.'

Peter was perplexed by her reply, deciding she was probably in shock. 'Are you ready? I could do it for you, save you this gruesome sight,' said her brother.

'No, I am ready; do you know I hated him? He was a bully and a coward!' spat out Bethany. Her brother was shocked by her violent tone. She advanced towards the door where her husband's body lay; Peter quickly followed, staying close. The room was bare and cold; Bethany gathered her coat about her tightly, and she lost her courage all of a sudden. The doctor in attendance stood gravely, nodding in deference as she entered. His body was covered by a sheet; she could see his feet sticking out at the end, and one foot was black and turned in an unnatural direction.

'Are you ready, Lady Rains?'

'Yes Doctor.'

Bethany gasped when she saw her husband's face; Peter moved forward and grabbed her arm for support. He too found the sight unnerving. Bethany nodded her head in confirmation, then quickly turned on her heel and left the room. Once outside she took a deep breath; so did her brother, relieved to be out of there. Peter suggested they go to church to pray and find comfort; Bethany's prayers, though, were not for her husband's soul — they were thanks for her freedom.

At the funeral, hidden under her veil, no tears were shed for the husband she hated, and her mind turned quickly to thinking about her new future without him. All of Max's wealth passed to her and she decided to live alone for the rest of her life, never to marry again. From the day Maximillian's heart stopped beating, the ravens never returned to the rowan tree … their job was done. The tree grew into a splendid specimen and it was one of Bethany's favourite trees in the garden.

*   *   *

The jeweller who bought the raven necklace knew its value as soon as he saw it, but he cunningly cast doubt on its authenticity and did not pay Lord Rains its true worth. Goldman the jeweller then set about researching the piece, asking the many contacts he had in the trading communities of Europe.

It took many years to gather information about the necklace, which the jeweller had hidden in a wall socket in his home. Its origins were ancient, as he had recognised the moment he saw it, and that it had been made by a master craftsman. Finally he discovered that it was made in England around the time of the Romans and the black amber had come from Russia. He also found out that the necklace supposedly possessed magical powers that were awakened by blood, but Goldman's mind was only concerned with its worth and nothing else. Those stories are rubbish ... but he'd use it anyway. People pay more money with those kinds of myths. If he

found the right buyer, he might be able to retire —
he was getting too old for all of this!

Gloucester, 1733

Goldman did find a buyer eventually: a Welsh merchant named Williams, very wealthy, who wanted it for his new, young wife. He was sure his wife would be enchanted with the piece and the mythical story associated with it. He treated Goldman in a supercilious manner, so the jeweller inflated the price even more and was able to retire with the money from the sale. Stupid little man had more money than sense.

The merchant was thrilled when he saw the joy

on his wife's face; it had cost him a pretty penny, but she was worth it, and she showed her gratitude in the most pleasurable way.

'Oh husband, the necklace is so beautiful; my grandmamma told me stories about ravens when I was growing up. There is an Irish Goddess who takes the form of this bird; she is associated with fertility. Thank you my love.' Aderyn winked, and then kissed her husband again, making him beam with pleasure. She loved her kindly husband very much; it was hard to resist a man who worshipped the very ground you walked on.

Aderyn wore the necklace every day. The black stone looked so cold, but always warmed her skin. She would touch the bird's shape, feeling the feathers so skilfully carved, and trace the gold filigree design. It made her dream of her homeland in Wales.

Robert Williams and his wife Aderyn dutifully attended church every Sunday in Gloucester. Bishop Lester was always fawning in his approach to any of his wealthy parishioners; he made

Aderyn's skin crawl whenever she touched his hand, or caught his gaze wandering over her body. She never mentioned to her husband how she felt, as it would seem wicked to have such thoughts. She wasn't going to wear her necklace to church this day, as she knew the church frowned upon anything remotely pagan, but the thought of having it around her neck made her smile with mischief. 'I wonder what Bishop Lester would think of this … lecherous old man.'

Aderyn waited quietly while her husband greeted the bishop; she smiled sweetly at him when he acknowledged her, and saw the lust in his beady eyes as he looked at her. She shuddered at the thought of this man touching her; his hands were large but effeminate, while his body was thick-set, muscular and strong. He frightened her. Aderyn knew there was nothing holy about this man, but he had many powerful friends, so she hid her thoughts behind her smile. She accidently dropped her kerchief and quickly bent to pick it up; the necklace fell from her bodice, and as she stood up Aderyn knew the bishop had seen it. For a fleeting moment a malicious expression showed on his face, but quickly it was gone and replaced by the pious façade he usually wore. Aderyn was glad to move away and find a seat.

'Are you feeling well, my dear? You feel cold all of a sudden.' Robert looked at his wife with concern.

'I am fine my dearest, just keep hold of my hand,' said Aderyn in a cheerful voice.

Bishop Lester stood at the pulpit, resplendent in his robes, bellowing his sermon. 'Keep guard, those of you with the true faith — protect your wives' and daughters' honour, and beware the work of wicked, fallen women. Amen.'

Bishop Lester's face had grown red with his vitriolic speech full of hell fire and self-righteousness; some of the more fanatical believers stared at him with adoration. Most of the congregation, particularly the women, looked uncomfortable. Aderyn wondered if the other women had the same feeling about the bishop, and she was glad when it was finished and she could stand outside in the sunshine.

In a couple of days, her husband would be leaving on one of his business trips. Aderyn did not travel with her husband, as it was the man's domain and she would find it tedious. But there was also another reason she would not be going; she had just learned she was pregnant with their first child, and her husband fussed over her terribly. He had sent for her cousin to come and keep her company, but unfortunately she was ill.

Aderyn assured him everything would be fine. 'Our housekeeper Mary is a sensible woman, my dear, so is Lady Anne next door. Your business is important and we will need the money with a child coming, so go and do not worry. I will send word if there are any troubles.' Aderyn smiled at her husband and kissed him on the cheek.

'If you feel you can spare me for a week or so, I will leave tomorrow. I shall bring you back something special,' said Robert as he kissed her hand.

A summons arrived from the bishop two days

after Robert left; Aderyn was resting when the maid brought in the letter. She looked at the seal and realised who it was from — it was addressed to Robert, but he wasn't here, so she carefully opened it and read the contents.

14th Day of April 1733

Dear Mr Williams,

I am writing to you with the authority of our Holy Church of England. It is concerning a certain necklace I observed your wife Aderyn was wearing at church last Sunday. The church frowns heavily upon any pagan worship and idolatry, and this piece of jewellery needs to be brought forward for my sanction.

I know you are a sensible man of true faith and I wish to protect your interests morally and financially. Also, I wish to ensure your wife understands the behaviour expected in our parish and avoid any unpleasant ramifications that could ensue.

Please believe your soul may be in peril if the church's teachings are not upheld, but I know you will follow the true path and I expect to see you in the afternoon on Wednesday with your wife. Please bring the piece of jewellery in question.

God bless you

Bishop Lester

Aderyn sat, holding the letters and fuming. *How dare he, it's none of his business … I knew he saw it. I'll see him myself; it was my fault for wearing it and Robert won't be back for another few days.*

Aderyn went on the requested day; she took one of her maids, asking her to get some shopping and telling her she would send for a carriage later. She entered the church hesitantly, but it was empty; she wondered where the bishop was as she walked slowly toward the altar lit with candles. Her footsteps echoed in the silent cathedral, and an oppressive feeling descended upon her, so she pulled her cape more tightly around herself. Aderyn stood waiting, feeling very alone now and regretting her decision to come.

The bishop stood hidden, watching Aderyn as she walked towards the altar. His beady eyes raked over her body, clad in a crème velvet dress with rose pink trimmings. He could see the creamy skin of her bosom above her neckline; he felt himself grow hard with desire. *She torments me with her beauty — she is a witch for sure, and she will burn in hell for tempting me.* The bishop could not believe the woman had the audacity to come alone. It was another sign of an ungodly woman.

He appeared from a side door, making Aderyn jump with fright. *I mustn't let this man intimidate me, but I really wish Robert was here now.*

'Lady Williams, welcome, where is your husband? I was looking forward to seeing you both, but your company will be just fine. Did you bring the necklace?' The bishop used a conciliatory tone of voice.

'Oh, Bishop Lester, you started me. Robert is away on business, but I decided to see you myself. I know Robert wouldn't mind, he trusts my judgement to make decisions when he is away. And yes, I brought the necklace, it's here,' said Aderyn, showing him a leather purse.

'Please, come to my inner sanctuary, no one will disturb us. I made sure we could discuss this matter in private.'

Aderyn followed obediently, ignoring the warning signals. He wouldn't dare do anything. They sat down as the bishop poured tea for them; Aderyn made small talk, commenting on the beauty of the stained glass windows adorning the church. The bishop enjoyed listening to the praise coming from Aderyn's lips … which he longed to kiss.

'May I see the necklace, please?'

Aderyn pushed the purse towards him and watched him as he studied the necklace eagerly, then suddenly put it down as if it had burnt his fingers. His demeanour changed suddenly. 'I feel it is best if you relinquish this possession to me. It is of pagan origin and unsuitable for you to be wearing it, especially in church.'

'But … it was a gift from my husband … and I am fond of it,' she replied earnestly.

'It is not your place to question any ruling from the church,' said the bishop haughtily.

Aderyn stood up. She could not hide her dislike for this man any longer and her face flushed with anger; she made ready to leave. 'I will discuss it with my husband when he returns; could I please have it back? I am leaving now.'

'No, it will stay with me, or I will report your behaviour as unseemly to your husband. A woman's reputation is vital — or do you think yourself above these things because of your husband's wealth?'

'How dare you. I would say it is your behaviour that could be brought to question,' said Aderyn defiantly.

'And what is that supposed to mean? Are you threatening me?' He said.

'I have seen the way you look at women in the church … the lust in your eyes, that's very unseemly,' said Aderyn, wanting to goad him now.

The bishop stood, his face flushed. He grabbed at Aderyn, who now was heading for the door. He was surprisingly quick for his size; he latched onto her wrist and pulled her back to him. Aderyn resisted with all her strength, but he was too strong.

'You witch; you have driven me to this.'

The bishop grabbed her face roughly and kissed her, Aderyn pulled away with disgust, so he slapped her face hard, making her lip bleed. She gasped in pain and fear, tasting the blood; she put her hands to her mouth and wiped the blood away. Aderyn saw the necklace on the table and grabbed it, smudging her blood onto the stone. This enraged the bishop even more, so he pushed her onto the table, cups and plates crashing to the floor. He ripped her dress from her shoulders and started pawing her breasts.

Aderyn fought hard, trying to scratch him, so he hit her again, dazing her for a brief moment. He then lifted her skirts, forcing her legs apart; Aderyn tried to knee him, so he punched her in the stomach and winded her. All she could think of now was her baby as he roughly entered her and fulfilled his need. She turned her head away from him the whole time, and she could not bear to watch his face grow red with his heaving efforts.

When his weight was finally lifted from her, she thought of the necklace she was clutching. She was squeezing it so tight, the carved surface had cut into her palm. Her fight returned and she struck him in the face with the black stone. Aderyn caught his cheek and cut it deeply; he did not expect such retaliation and was shocked at first. Then he felt the pain, turning his lust into a violent rage. *I need to destroy her for good — all the sin is hers, not mine.* His wrapped his large hands around her neck and choked her until she lay still.He stared at her lifeless body for a moment, then the reality of what he had done hit him.

I will lose everything over this witch, I could hang, I will have to dispose of her body quickly and think of some story … no one would dare question me.

The bishop tidied himself, washing his cut cheek and applying some salve to it; he would say he tripped and fell after feeling dizzy. He ogled over Aderyn's body once more before wrapping it in a sheet, making sure she was wearing the necklace; he paused for a moment and looked at her lovely face, framed by her dark curls. *She is still beautiful, even in death … the witch.* He hid her body in the church and summoned a lad he knew who would dump her body in the river for a fee. Also, there were plenty of gypsies about he could blame for the murder.

That afternoon, Aderyn's maid, Mary came scurrying into the church, frantic because her mistress had not returned. The bishop pretended he was busy with another matter and left her waiting, preparing himself for what he was going to say to her.

'Please pardon me Bishop, but the Lady

Williams came to see you this morning and has not returned home. We are now so worried, did you see her? And she is with child … this is terrible.'

The bishop flinched on hearing she was expecting a child … he would have to do more penance for God's forgiveness. 'Oh, good Lord, this is disturbing news — Lady Williams was here only briefly, hours ago, but I told her I would see her next week when her husband returned, as I thought it more appropriate. I was surprised that she had ventured out alone; it is not safe on the streets. These are ungodly times, you must call the constable immediately. I will leave my work and escort you there,' he said with a concerned expression.

'Oh Bishop, you are too kind, I feel faint with worry. Thank you so much, I apologise for interrupting God's work. I'm sure she has just been delayed by a friend, and it is just a misunderstanding.' The maid kept wringing her hands and curtsying, which annoyed the bishop … stupid woman.

The constable's office was not far, but the

bishop strode ahead and Mary had to almost run to keep up with him, and was breathless when she arrived. The bishop also had to acknowledge the many greetings he received from the townsfolk as he walked along; it made him feel confident and above the law.

The constable was a straight-talking honest man and he attended church every week, so when they arrived they were shown straight in, and the bishop let the maid do the talking.

'Calm yourself woman, get your breath back and start from the beginning,' said the burly constable. The bishop stood quietly, keeping a calm appearance, and when asked about Aderyn he answered nonchalantly, giving the impression that he only spoke briefly to her as he was too busy. The constable wrote everything down and called to his men to search around the church and town.

'Constable Fallon, I don't wish to make assumptions or cast doubt upon anyone, but there are gypsies down near the river and about the town. A lady alone would be very vulnerable to such unscrupulous people such as these,' said the bishop, feigning concern.

'Yes Bishop, I am aware of these people, but we need to find evidence before we can convict someone. Did Lady Williams say where she was going when you dismissed her?'

'No, but I assumed a carriage would be sent to take her home. I feel I have been neglectful,' said the bishop contritely.

'No Bishop, you are a busy man. Thank you for alerting us. Mary, go back to your duties, we will take over from here. Oh, and Master Williams is away? Word must be sent to him immediately.'

'Yes, certainly,' said the maidservant, curtsying.

Robert Williams received word the next day and left within the hour; his mind was filled with dread and uncertainty over his wife, and he called to the driver for the horses to go faster.

✳   ✳   ✳

Bishop Lester chose one of the homeless boys who

63

slept near the church to do his dirty work. This particular lad was strong but deficient of mind … perfect, he would do the bishop's bidding without question. He was promised extra food, a blanket and some coins for his efforts. Bishop Lester brought the body to the back door of the church, as he did not want the filthy beggar inside his rooms — his stench was unbearable.

'Samuel, come here my son. I have something which needs to be thrown in the river. Make sure no one sees you, or you will be in trouble; drop it where the current will take it away. And one more thing — unwrap the sheet and get rid of it so no one will find it. Do not be alarmed at what you see, lad, evil can take many forms … can I trust you to do God's work, Samuel? I will reward you well.' The bishop put on one of his kindest smiles as he said this.

The young man nodded in agreement. His only thought was for his reward, and he was afraid of the bishop; he knew how cruel he could be, and had the scars on his back to prove it, so he would do exactly what he wanted. He picked up Aderyn's body easily and picked his way through the church graveyard, heading for the river. The sky was cloudy, obscuring the light of the moon, but Samuel knew the way by heart, as he had dumped other things in the river before at night time. No one was about on this cold night, not even on the bridge above, so Samuel made his way down the embankment close to the stone pylons and laid down his load. He could hear the sound of the fast flowing water, and caught the unpleasant smell of some of the debris floating along with the current.

The clouds suddenly parted and the moon shone brightly, lighting up the night sky as he unravelled the sheet and stared in shock at the woman he now saw, lifeless, but still so beautiful. He knew he was not supposed to look at her, but he had never been so close to someone who looked so clean and who wore such expensive clothes. He tentatively leant down and touched her hand; it had blood on it, and so did her face. He touched her dark hair and felt a strange sensation come over him. He started to cry… why did someone so beautiful have to die and be thrown in the river? *I do not understand anything of this world, or of God.*

Samuel then noticed the necklace hanging around her neck. He lifted it up; the moonlight shone on its surface. He wanted to take it, but he didn't want to make the bishop angry and he knew he should get back … Samuel didn't want to keep him waiting. He picked up Aderyn's body easily and threw it into the river; he watched as she was taken away by the current and disappeared from view. The clouds gathered again, obscuring the moon's light. Samuel stood in darkness as he wiped away his tears and gathered up the sheet. He ripped it into smaller strips before dumping it into a channel which served as an open sewer for the town, then ran all the way back to the church.

He knocked on the door and waited; he started shivering, so he hugged his ragged coat more tightly around himself. Eventually he heard footsteps; the giant bolt was slid back and the door opened, but it was another priest who answered the door. Samuel did not know him and was wary, but he seemed kindly enough.

'Good evening my son, I am Father John. Bishop Lester has taken to his bed early. Bless you and take these gifts for your work.'

The priest gave him some coins and food. Later he went to sleep with a full stomach and a warm blanket, deciding the world wasn't such a bad place after all. He didn't question the work he did for the church when they rewarded him so well, and the bishop assured him of his place in heaven.

✳   ✳   ✳

Aderyn's body was found two days later, upstream amongst the weeds; she was spotted from the bridge by one of the constable's men. It was a sorry sight for the men who found her; she was well known for her beauty, which was now destroyed.

Robert had questioned the maidservant Mary upon arrival; she was distraught and couldn't stop crying, but her master was a kindly man and he assured her as best he could. He then went to the bishop, who told him everything possible was being done, and that he was praying for him and his wife.

When Robert arrived back home, the constable was waiting for him. Robert steeled himself for the news … but he sank into a chair when he heard what had happened to his beloved wife. The constable gripped his shoulder and held back his own tears. Robert just sat, staring — he felt numb and it was hard to breathe. Mary started wailing in the background but Robert didn't notice.

'We will find the culprit, I assure you — and my sincerest condolences to you sir. Oh, and before I forget, your wife had this necklace tangled in her hair. I knew you would want to have it.' The constable placed it in Robert's hand, who stared down at it without replying.

'It is late now sir, so you can come tomorrow to formally identify the body. Take care sir and God bless you,' said the constable as he left the house; his heart was heavy as he made his way through the town.

Robert did not sleep much that night. He sat in a chair, staring into the fire that Mary kept going until she was too exhausted and went to bed. Robert woke up with the sun; his muscles ached and his mind was dull with the lack of sleep. He refused any breakfast and dressed himself mechanically, knowing what was ahead of him this horrible day.

His legs felt like lead and the warmth of the sunshine did not lift his spirits as he walked to the police station. He was greeted by the constable quietly and taken to the room where his beloved wife's body laid cold and dead. As he entered the room, he covered his face and gasped when he saw his wife's swollen face and bruised neck. For the first time a terrible anger grew in him; he clenched his fists, and he wanted to kill whoever did this. He identified his wife's body and then strode from the room.

People moved out of his way when they saw the anger blazing in his eyes. He walked for miles, not really knowing where he was heading, and then he ended up in a drinking house and drank himself into oblivion. The constable sent someone to follow him and bring him home safely.

Aderyn had a private funeral; Bishop Lester did the service efficiently and promised Aderyn's soul would be in heaven. He was sure his penance was sufficient to absolve his wrongdoing in the eyes of God, and he felt calm during the service. Robert sat stony-faced, not really listening to the service or believing in God's mercy; he had not eaten much in the last few days and felt unsure about his own will to live. He was comforted by his family, who were shocked at his thoughts, but prayed for him and God's mercy upon his suffering.

Robert had spared no expense for Aderyn's gravestone: it was made from polished granite and had an ornately carved raven as the centrepiece. He made sure fresh flowers were placed everyday where she lay. Robert kept the necklace by his bedside, holding it often; it gave him comfort as it warmed his fingers, and he knew how much his wife loved it.

Robert asked the bishop about the letter he sent concerning the necklace and what he wanted done with the piece.

'You have suffered enough, my son. I will forget I ever saw the necklace, I know you meant no disrespect. Keep it as a memento of your wife,' said the bishop patronisingly.

'You have been so thoughtful Bishop, it has helped me greatly,' said Robert sincerely.

'Do they have any suspects?' the bishop asked.

'Yes, they are questioning a man at the moment … the evil amongst us astounds me and tests my faith in God,' said Robert, looking at the ground, sounding defeated.

'The ways of God are a mystery to us, but know we must trust in him always,' said the bishop as he made the sign of the cross over Robert.

Some unfortunate gypsy was tried and convicted for Aderyn's murder; he had no defence and no money, and the townspeople were glad to see the culprit brought to justice. Robert went to see the hanging — a gruesome spectacle. The crowd was unruly and jeered, and he took a long time to die, with his body jerking as he fought for his last breaths. Robert felt nauseous from the cruelty and the smell of so many unwashed bodies pressing in on him, but for a moment it did bring Robert some sense of justice.

He couldn't help thinking how the murder made no sense. She had no money with her, she was still wearing the necklace … gypsies steal things, don't they? Why did she go without me? It was just a necklace, and now she has lost her life.

So he threw himself into his work and became very wealthy. He used some of the money to establish a school for orphan girls, where they could receive an education and skills to make a better life for themselves. He moved to the north of England years later and finally remarried; his new wife was not as beautiful as Aderyn, but was a kind and cheery soul named Anne. They had a daughter named Sarah. Her father gave his only daughter the necklace when she turned sixteen, and she thought it was very beautiful, but something about it disturbed her. She was a god-fearing young woman and thought the necklace improper somehow. But it also intrigued her; she would hold it and feel its warmth seep into her fingers, and daydream about an imaginary lover which made her blush. Sarah was never told about the woman it belonged to, as Robert resolved to never speak of Aderyn again, not even to his wife.

✳   ✳   ✳

Three months had passed since Aderyn's death and the bishop now felt safe that the truth would never be discovered. It had been a fine day and the bishop's favourite place was at the top of the church, high above the city — it gave him a sense of power up there. He climbed the stairs as quickly as he could, eager to see the sun setting; he was breathing hard when he reached the top and the sweet air was wonderful to take in. He felt like a mighty king standing up there, looking past the city rooftops to the fields beyond, the colours softened by the setting sun. He stood breathing deeply and calmness settled over him; the city looked and smelt cleaner from up here away from the filthy populace below. He was so caught up in his own thoughts that he didn't notice the three raven sisters, the *tri Morrignae*, perched nearby and watching him … not until they launched their attack.

The triune Goddesses, the three daughters,
the famous war furies have been unleashed.
Sources of bitter fighting
Were the three daughters of Ernmas

(*Goddess of Battle*, R A Macalister 1941)

The bishop heard the flutter of feathers. As he turned, one of the birds went straight for his eyes; the two other birds attacked his hands as they wildly thrashed about, trying to protect himself. He tried to grab the birds and pull them off, but they were big, strong and hungry for revenge. They pecked cruelly, tearing at his flesh; the bishop was staggering about with pain and confusion. One of his eyes was nearly out already. The emptiness in his skull where his eye once sat was raw with pain, and the eyeball slapped into his face, hanging by a sinew as he fought hard to save himself.

He yelled out for help but he was so high up, no one heard. His fingers were now bloody strips. One raven started on his other eye; its claws gripped his face, digging into his flesh, its sharp beak tearing the eyeball out and dropping it on the flagstones.

Blinded now and in terrible pain, the bishop had lost all sense of direction; his robes were covered in blood and his mind was in total confusion. He ran about wildly before toppling over the side of the church to the ground below. He realised his fate with horror as he hurtled towards his death, yelling with fear before his body smashed like a watermelon onto the street. His body was twisted into an unnatural shape and a large pool of blood formed around the body, following the cracks in the pavement.

A woman screamed in horror, and soon a

crowd gathered, some crossing themselves at such a demonic sight. The three ravens sat on the edge of the church tower, croaking loudly to each other as they picked the flesh from their claws and preened their feathers. No one noticed them as they flew into the growing darkness and disappeared.

The bishop's death was seen as a tragic accident; he was buried with great expense and had an extensive sermon which praised his godliness. It was attended by many important people, but in truth most of the townspeople felt no real sorrow for the man, and they hoped for a better replacement.

Manchester, England, 1765

Sarah knew her father was dying. He had grown so thin and he couldn't keep any food down. Sometimes the pain overtook him, and the doctor had to be called. Apparently it was some kind of growth in his stomach; the doctor could feel a hard lump and they had nothing to cure it. She loved him so much; he was such a kindly man and was good to her mother, and he made sure Sarah had received a good education, which was rare in those times. Sarah had a strong sense of her self-worth and had no desire to marry, which vexed her mother and caused a rift between them. But Sarah wanted to teach, and promised her father she would carry on his work in educating young girls. But for now, all her time was used to care for him and help her mother.

This day had been particularly bad for Robert. The pain was getting worse and he was getting weaker; he refused any food or water. He told Sarah to bring the necklace to him and that he had something to tell her that was very important, so she went to get it and waited for her father to speak. He opened his eyes and took the necklace, holding it close to his chest, and began to cry.

'My dearest child, this necklace is very special … it belonged to my first wife, her name was Aderyn. She was so beautiful, but she died so young. Your mother doesn't even know about her … she was murdered by a vagabond when I was away on business many years ago, when I lived in Gloucester. But you know, I have always wondered about the circumstances of her death …'

Robert's mind seemed to wander then. He

stared out of the window as if remembering something, and Sarah wiped the tears away from her father's face, shocked now by what he was saying. 'Father, you must rest,' said Sarah anxiously.

'No ... I have never spoken of this and I want to tell you before I die. Your mother is a good woman, look after her for me, but I have never loved her like Aderyn and I feel ashamed of this. Know that I have loved you most of all, my dear daughter. Forgive me my sin against your mother ... please.'

'Of course Father ... love is a strange thing ... and you have been so good to us,' said Sarah as she bent and kissed his cheek. He was so cold now and his breathing was laboured; she got up to fetch a priest, but he gripped her hand, pulling her back.

'No priest ... if God really exists, I'll take my chances.' And with that, he relaxed his grip and died.

'Father ... Father ... oh no, no.' Sarah lay on his frail chest and sobbed. Her mother came running, but she was too late. Sarah never told her what her father had said before he died; it would serve no purpose now.

Sarah stood at her father's graveside, watching the coffin being lowered into the ground; her mother clung to her, sobbing quietly. It had started to rain in the gloomy churchyard. Sarah had worn the necklace to the funeral; it gave her comfort and felt warm against her heart. She couldn't stop thinking about it after what her father had told her; she felt a bit guilty wearing it when she thought of her mother. *Love is so untrue. I will never marry.*

Sarah continued her father's work and was well respected in the town; she was now twenty-one years old and should have been married by conventional standards. One day, she decided to visit Aderyn's grave; it would be a big trip and she would have to travel with her maid and a footman. She had the financial means to travel well, so it would be an exciting adventure for such a young woman travelling without a husband. Sarah had researched her father and the town of Gloucester where he'd lived; she had also written to the church authorities to confirm where Aderyn was buried.

Her mother complained bitterly about the trip, saying that she should have a family of her own by now, but Sarah held her nerve and told her mother she would be visiting other orphanages to see the conditions there.

'I don't know what your father would think of this trip, Sarah,' said her mother, exasperated.

Sarah didn't answer. *I wonder, Mother, if you ever really knew what Father thought.*

Sarah was so excited to be away from home and took everything in — her world had expanded. Walking around Gloucester made her think about her father as a young man and the woman he loved so dearly. Sarah visited the church and got directions to the grave. She stood there, reading the inscription on the gravestone, and was shocked that it included an unborn baby ... *how terrible, she was with child.* Then she noticed the carving of a raven identical to her necklace and realised she had been holding it unconsciously. The grave was well tended, with fresh flowers. This puzzled her, so she went and asked the priest, who explained that her father made provision for the grave to be tended, and fresh flowers placed on it, until such time there are no more funds available. Sarah was astounded at her father's gesture, and thought it very romantic.

Sarah sought out a reputable jeweller in Gloucester and sold the necklace. She felt it belonged to a part of her father's life that would always be separate from her and her mother, and she put the money into her charities for young women, sure that her father would have approved. When Sarah returned home, she continued working and remained unmarried until she was twenty-five, and considered an old spinster. One of the local businessmen had been patiently courting Sarah for three years until she finally believed in his sincerity, and (to the joy of her mother) she finally married. They had a long happy marriage together, although it produced no children, but Sarah thought of the girls in her charities as her daughters.

The jeweller was thrilled with his purchase; he never thought a piece made with such skill would come his way. All he needed now was the right buyer.One day, Alexander Gruzinsky walked through the door; he was a merchant from Odessa. His fine clothes showed he was a man of means and the jeweller welcomed Alexander warmly when he entered his shop.

'Good day to you sir, please let me know if I can be of any assistance today,' said Mr Jacobs, bowing and smiling.

'*Zdravstvuyte* … hello, I want to buy presents for my wife and daughter,' said Alexander with a deep voice, smiling as he inspected the jewellery.

Jacobs watched quietly. He did not speak Russian, but at least this man could speak fair English. 'Is there anything in particular? A ring or … necklace perhaps,' said Jacobs hopefully.

'Necklace would be nice for my daughter; she is to marry when I return home. Maybe a ring for my wife though.' Jacobs brought out the jet necklace and saw the surprise on the merchant's face when he inspected it. 'Ah, I'm sure this stone is from Russia. We call it black amber, it is very well crafted and the gold is of good quality. Do you know its history?' said Alexander, very interested now.

'Yes, the stone is from Russia, here in England we call it jet. The chain is made from Welsh gold, and I know it is of Celtic design and is a very old piece sir,' said Jacobs enthusiastically.

'Mm … it is very beautiful, and I like that ring there, the sapphire, could I look at that one also?'

Jacobs quickly got the ring out, talking the piece up as much as possible; it would be a very profitable day indeed if he could sell them both.

'Ah, the ring is my wife's size too, which is fortunate as I have to leave this afternoon. I will take both if we can come to an agreement on the price,' said Alexander, knowing the jeweller was keen to make a sale. Jacobs soon discovered Alexander was a very astute buyer and knew the value of the pieces, but finally was thrilled with the sale and the price they agreed upon. He took extra care wrapping the gifts, using the best jewellery cases he had for this valued customer.

'*Bal'shoye spaseeba* … thank you very much Mr Jacobs, they will be two very happy women when they receive these presents,' said Alexander, lifting his hat as he passed the jeweller, who held the door open for him to pass.

'Thank you kindly, my dear sir. Good health to you and your family, and best wishes for your daughter's wedding,' Jacobs answered sincerely, bowing to Alexander.

Alexander Gruzinsky returned home to a welcoming family. His wife Raisa was thrilled with her sapphire ring and his daughter Natalya was enchanted with the necklace. She threw her arms around her father's neck and kissed him, saying he was the only man she would ever really love.

'Ah come Natalya, you are marrying a wonderful man in Patryk,' said Alexander, holding her at arm's length while pretending to be stern and serious.

'Oh Papa, I know, it's just that I love you the

most,' said Natalya, dancing away while looking at the necklace.

His eldest daughter was due to be married in three weeks, but she was such a dreamer and so naïve in many ways. Her parents worried that she wouldn't be prepared for the responsibilities of marriage and having children of her own; she was always writing stories and daydreaming about something or other. Natalya was to marry into a Polish family and move to Warsaw once she was married — her future husband was a soldier named Patryk Wis'nieski.

The wedding day finally came and it was wonderful; the vodka flowed and the couple were a good match. Natalya wanted to look like a fairy tale princess and her parents gave her the dream: her dark hair was pinned back with a diamanté tiara, and her dress had a pearl bodice. She wore satin shoes and a full veil that sparkled under the lights. Her bouquet was made of tiny blue, yellow and pink flowers with a gold ribbon. The groom looked very handsome decked out in his military uniform, and his friends from his brigade formed a guard of honour.

Warsaw, Poland, 1768

Natalya settled into her marriage well and was soon pregnant; the old midwife Agnieszka, who attended the births in her area, saw the necklace around Natalya's neck and recognised its significance. Although she was Catholic and went to church each week, Agnieszka was taught about the old gods and their powers by her grandmother as she was growing up, and she still believed in them.

She asked Natalya if she could look at the necklace; she held it reverently, admiring the beauty of the craftsmanship. 'This is a symbol of protection for women in childbirth, my girl. It has great power, you must wear it when the time comes, yeah,' said Agnieszka seriously.

Natalya hugged the old lady warmly, kissing her wrinkled cheek, liking her very much for her kindness. 'Whatever you say, Aggie. My father bought it for me in England, it was a wedding present. It's one of my favourites. I knew there was something special about it.'

When Natalya went into labour, the midwife made sure she was wearing the necklace. It was a long labour and Natalya was growing weaker by the hour. Agnieszka had grown fond of Natalya; she was a sweet girl, but a little naïve and, as with all new mothers, totally unprepared for the rigours of childbirth. Natalya gripped Agnieszka's hand so hard the midwife felt like calling out, but she stayed, willing Natalya on. The other hand held the necklace, squeezing it when the pain was at its worst, leaving an imprint in her palm. The sweat ran down her face as she strained with effort; she thought she was going to die. Just when she could bear it no more, the baby was born and Natalya collapsed into her pillows.

'Ah, Natalya, you have a healthy son!' Agnieszka exclaimed proudly. She was so relieved it was over for the young woman, and carefully laid the little wrinkled bundle on Natalya's chest. His first cry energised Natalya and she couldn't stop crying and smiling. Agnieszka hugged her, then went about helping Natalya finish the birth. 'You did well, my girl … see, the necklace helped you,' said Agnieszka sagely.

Natalya ended up having many children: six girls and three boys, who all lived into adulthood. Her last child was born in 1792. By then Natalya was at a very precarious age to give birth; people in the neighbourhood began to whisper that she must practice witchcraft to still be able to have children, and they thought she looked remarkably young for her age. Even the local priest became involved when he heard the rumours, but he could find no such happenings and gave

Natalya a special blessing for the safe delivery of her child.

Natalya knew it was the necklace that enabled her to survive, though she couldn't explain it. And in a couple of months, after a quick labour a baby girl was born. Natalya named her Sonia; she was special to Natalya, as she knew she would probably be her last child.

Natalya took months to recover from the birth and the doctor said her heart was weakened by the labour. She lived another eight years cherishing her little daughter, who reminded her of herself as a child and gave her much joy. Before she died, Natalya bequeathed the raven necklace to Sonia for her sixteenth birthday; she also wrote a note to her daughter telling her how important the necklace is and how it must be kept in the family.

Patryk never remarried; he got live-in help to look after the family and home, and spent as much time as he could with his children. Sonia loved him very much, but she missed her mother terribly. She would often hold the necklace, feeling its warmth and admiring its beauty; it made her feel close to her mother.

Sonia married at eighteen and had four children, three boys and one girl, and always wore the necklace during childbirth. They all continued to live in Lodz, Poland, which become a very prosperous city through its textile industries. The necklace stayed in the family for over a hundred years; it became a precious family heirloom, being passed down through the female line from Natalya.

York, England, 1910

Natalya's descendent, Halina, was very bright at school and was sent to Switzerland to study, graduating from the University of Zurich as a teacher. She had a passion for English history and language, and wanted to see more of the world, so she accepted a teaching position in the city of York, England. She was the first of her family to leave Poland, but times had changed for women in this bright new world of the twentieth century; they were being educated and slowly liberated from their traditional roles. In some countries they even had the vote.

Halina settled into her new life well, and in York she was surrounded with all the history anyone could wish for. It was founded by the Romans; there had also been a large Viking settlement there, then called Jorvik.

In her spare time, Halina travelled around the city, learning everything about its history. During one of these trips, she met a man named Sean Percy. Halina went to buy some lunch and started chatting to him while waiting for her order; he was charming and funny, and he had the most incredible blue eyes. They ended up having lunch together and decided to meet again. Sean was an engineer with the railways and he got to travel all over England; he promised to show Halina all the best places in the British Isles. His parents lived near Dublin; his father was Irish and his mother Welsh.

Halina had only had one close girlfriend since arriving in York, a fellow teacher, but she had never socialised much with men other than her brothers back home and other students in her class. Most of them were very studious and Halina had only been friends with them, never feeling anything romantic towards them. She had never met a man like Sean before; he seemed very confident with girls, and soon Halina fell in love for the first time.

They travelled to Ireland to meet Sean's parents. His mother was very sweet but his father seemed very stern towards Sean, although he made Halina feel welcome. He was their only son and his father seemed to expect much from him.

When Sean asked Halina to marry him, she happily agreed.

Sean met with Halina's parents and they approved of him, and the fact that they were of the same faith made things easier between the families. They had not known each other long, but were now going to become husband and wife. The service was able to be held at Lodz Cathedral, which made the family and Halina very happy. They had always wanted her to be married in this historic old church, where many other family members had been married in the past.

It was a beautiful old church and the sun shone softly through the stained glass windows during the service. Most of the family attended from both sides and it was a joyous day. Halina looked beautiful; she was so tiny, like a doll, and her long dark hair was pinned up with tiny jewelled flowers which sparkled in the soft light of the church. Her dress was of a simple design with delicate ivory lace, and her bouquet was of pink and crème roses. Sean wore a deep blue suit with a crème rose in the lapel. He felt like crying when he saw Halina, she looked so beautiful.

He would only have such a short time with his wife before he had to leave — every man had to do his duty.

Halina was given the raven necklace by her mother Lilliana before she left to go to her new home. Halina hugged her when she saw the gift;

she knew the significance of it from listening to all the stories told about the necklace by her mother and her grandmother. When she was a little girl, Halina used to ask her mother if she could hold it; the raven fascinated her. She used to pretend it was alive and could fly.

They had a short honeymoon in Wales and then Sean left for war. Their time together was brief, but it was the same for so many couples in those years of the Great War. Halina continued to work and help in the war effort, waiting for any letters from Sean. He was repatriated home in October 1917; he was shot in his lower left leg and received a head wound that left a scar near his hairline. He would have a permanent limp for the rest of his life. But the soldiers who returned also had scars that were hidden from view — damage to their minds that would never go away. Sean was luckier than most; his physical injuries didn't prevent him from going back to work, but like so many he came back a troubled man.

By the end of the war, Europe was destroyed and

the death toll was appalling — its peoples turned to the peace of nature for healing.

* * *

The Morrigan, Goddess of War, hooded crow of battle, would have been witness to human sacrifice like no other time, where men were slaughtered on an industrial scale by weapons of mass destruction and the land laid to waste and covered in blood. These men now lay in cemeteries with great monuments that record their names and honour their death, as she would have.

But like the Goddess, they did not die — their courage made them immortal.

* * *

England, 1919

Sean recovered from his wounds and found plenty of work after the war ended, which helped to keep him occupied and feel useful again. Halina gave him as much love and support as she could muster, and their relationship seemed to be happy enough. Halina had hopes of having a child soon, but so far nothing had happened, she had noticed Sean drinking more and becoming moody. She thought if they started a family it would help him.

One day Sean announced he wanted to go back

to Ireland to be near his parents; Halina wanted to keep the peace, so she agreed. They settled in Clontarf, near Dublin, in a lovely house with a view of the sea. The area was full of history and Halina felt excited now, seeing it as a new start to their lives.

Her parents helped financially, paying for most of the house to help the couple, especially since Sean had suffered in the war. Sean accepted their help gratefully but Halina knew Sean was a proud man and wanted to prove to everyone, especially his father, that he could support his family by himself. So Sarah kept working for now, until she could become a mother and stay at home looking after her family. In a couple of months, Halina did find out she was having a baby and was so excited to tell Sean. She cooked a special dinner for the occasion.

Sean was late coming home this night and Halina was getting anxious; she wanted to tell him about the baby. When he finally arrived home, she felt annoyed and angry as she opened the door. 'Where have you been? Your dinner is cold and I was worried,' Halina said accusingly instead of greeting him with the excitement she had felt earlier.

Sean looked annoyed and stepped inside, pushing past her. She slammed the door shut, making him turn in anger. 'I was down the pub with my work mates, one of them is leaving. We had a send-off. I work hard, woman, don't start nagging me as soon as I step in the door,' shouted Sean.

'Don't yell at me, I've been waiting here alone and your dinner is ruined, it's wasteful,' retorted Halina. It's what happened next that stunned Halina into silence; Sean advanced and slapped her hard across the face, making her lip bleed. It was such a shock; Halina just stood there holding her face, and she couldn't believe what he had done. Sean didn't apologise; he just turned and went into the bathroom. Halina slowly walked into the kitchen and sat down slowly, stunned and stared at the wall, listening to the clock tick loudly in the silence.

She could hear him running his bath. When he was finished, she went to the bathroom and locked the door, staring into the mirror. A bruise was already colouring her face; she started to cry. She undressed slowly and then slipped into the bath, letting the hot water relax and soothe her. She felt numb, and tried to justify his actions somehow, to try to understand what had happened. All the excitement of her pregnancy was lost in her confusion and fear. *When I tell him it will be alright, he'll be sorry, sometimes men are like that.*

When Halina got into bed, Sean was already asleep and snoring, Halina got into the sheets quietly, trying not to disturb him. She turned away from him, staring into the darkness, and it was a long time before she fell asleep.

The next morning, Sean was very apologetic and promised he would be home early and take Halina out to dinner for a treat. Halina was able to cover the bruise with make-up; they had a lovely time and all was forgiven. When Halina told him about the baby, he was so happy he picked her up and hugged her tightly, and he brought home some flowers the next night. The future seemed brighter for them now; Halina would often get the necklace out of her jewellery box and hold it, her thoughts turning to her family back home ... how she missed them and their support.

Sean had not acted violently again and she hadn't told anybody about it, especially her mother. Halina just put it down to the drink and him being in a bad mood. Sean was genuinely excited about becoming a father; he said that after seeing all that death in the war, it would be wonderful if they could create life.

One night as they lay in bed, he started talking about his childhood and his father; Halina had never heard him say much about his life before the war. 'I want to be a good father ... you know, understanding. I love my dad but he was so strict. He used to drink and become angry, I never felt I knew him ... we weren't close,' said Sean as he stared at the ceiling. Halina couldn't see his face in the dark, but he sounded sad and a bit resentful, so she held him close and hugged him. He fell asleep in her arms.

Unfortunately, Halina suffered a miscarriage; she was devastated and so was Sean. The nurses were very good to her and assured Halina that one day she would have a healthy baby. She used to listen to the nurses talking and joking as they did their work; she liked their accents, and some of them were slightly different to her husband's.

'Oh well, here's another lot for the Maggies,' laughed one of the nurses.

Halina did not understand what that meant and asked one of the nurses later when she came to take her blood pressure.

'Oh, you don't know? Well, they're what we call the women who work in the Magdalen Sisters' laundries, run by the Catholic Church. They're dotted all over Ireland. Sad places really, I heard some terrible rumours about them; apparently they're worked like slaves. They wash all the laundry from hospital, goals, mental institutions and the monasteries. But you won't have to worry, only unmarried mothers and ... you know, women who have fallen from grace, well, in the churches and society's eyes … are sent there. You rest now, best to keep your mind on happier things.' The nurse attended to another patient, then pushed the large trolley full of washing out into the hall.

Once upon a time, the warrior Goddess roamed the land, proud and free, revered and feared by all. One of her forms was the washer-at-the-ford, washing the clothes or armour of doomed warriors. She was seen as Badb, the beautiful young woman washing bloody clothes and keening.

But the new religion degraded the old gods and beliefs.

The work of washing clothes in the Magdalene laundries degraded and punished women, bringing much shame to them.

Halina thought about what the nurse had said and was sure she had passed one of those laundries on her way to work. It was a very foreboding place; the building looked like a prison, with a drab exterior and no garden, and bars on the window. Halina was born into a wealthy family and hadn't known much hardship, but she felt sad knowing that's how women were treated by an institution run by the church. Halina had noticed the fear in people of the church, very peculiar to Ireland; she had noticed it in her husband also. *I am so fortunate, and I should not feel sorry for myself — things will be alright with the next baby.*

Halina used to go to old bookstores in her spare time, looking mainly for history books about Ireland. One day she found a book about Irish myth and lore; she was fascinated with the stories and learnt about the Goddess 'M'orrioghain' and how she could be seen as a raven in one of her earthly forms. She looked at her necklace, beginning to believe that whoever made this was representing this goddess and that it truly must be very old and valuable … not that she would ever sell it. When she read the book, she would finger the necklace, and the stories and language would make her daydream about another life.

One night she was reading, engrossed in the words of her book, and didn't hear Sean come home; he stood at the doorway looking at Halina. She jumped up with fright when she saw him and noticed his expression.

'Hello dear … I see your head is stuck in a book again.'

'Hi Sean, I was just reading a bit waiting for you,' said Halina apologetically. 'Dinner is ready; I kept it warm for you.'

'I don't want it, I had dinner at the pub,' he replied in a surly voice.

'I'll have a wash then and go to bed … I'm tired,' said Halina as she went to leave. She could tell he was in a foul mood and wanted to avoid a confrontation.

'I haven't finished with you yet,' said Sean as he raised his arm, blocking the doorway. Halina froze, she could see he was really angry now and she knew that pain was coming. He grabbed her arm and wrenched it back, making her cry out; she could smell the alcohol on his breath as he tried to kiss her and she turned away. This enraged him more and he punched her in the face, making her nose bleed. Halina gasped in pain; her eyes started to water and she covered her face with her hands. 'Now you don't seem so high and mighty, do you?'

He grabbed her long hair, pulling it back, and then kissed her roughly; he didn't even care that blood was running down her face. Halina submitted meekly to prevent more violence from him, but Sean took this as a positive sign and dragged her by the arm into the bedroom, pushing her onto the bed and forcing himself inside her. When he was finished, Halina rolled away from him and curled into a protective ball, silent and hardly breathing. Sean stomped out and left, slamming the front door, and spent the night with his parents, making some excuse to them for why he had to stay over.

Halina slowly got up and washed herself, examining the damage done to her. Then she took some headache pills and went to bed. She lay in the darkness, staring at the wall and wondering what was happening to her life.

She took a few weeks off work. By then the marks would be gone and she wouldn't have to make excuses. Sean kept his distance and stayed at his friend's place for a couple of nights. He told his mate some story about her …but she didn't care anymore.

Halina used to go and sit at the docks, watching the ocean; she wished it would carry her away from this place forever. She loved the salt smell of the sea and watching the ships disappear from view, wondering where they went. Some days, if the weather was good, she would take some lunch and her book on Irish mythology, stare at the ever changing sea and dream about another life … one where her raven really could take flight, like she believed as a child, and fly her to a place where she would be truly loved.

Sean returned home a couple of days later, sober and terribly contrite. He had flowers and begged forgiveness, so again she forgave him. Their religion and vows did not allow divorce, so she would stay and try to make it work. Soon she discovered she was pregnant again, and she prayed that they would have a child to love together. Sean stopped drinking and again became attentive and gentle towards her, promising never to raise his hand to her again.

But fortune did not smile upon Halina; she had another miscarriage and she returned to her disintegrating life with Sean. The pattern of his drinking and violence continued and his threats became worse.

Halina kept most of this hidden, but her friend Christine sensed something was wrong. Once when they were at lunch, Christine cautiously broached the subject. 'Is everything going alright between you and Sean? I don't mean to pry but sometimes, especially lately, you seem anxious and a bit jumpy. Tell me to mind my own business if you like, but I'm worried about you,' Christina said as she reached out and gently squeezed Halina's hand.

Halina instantly broke down into tears and

told her friend all that had been happening in her marriage.

'You have got to leave him, eventually he'll kill you. My aunty died this way. He's been in the War … I'm not making excuses for him, but a lot of these returned soldiers have problems, you know what I mean. Go back to your family in Poland, you can work and support yourself. At least you'll be safe there. I know your mother will understand,' said Christine vehemently, trying to get through to Halina the danger she was in.

'Thanks, that has crossed my mind … I know you're right, but I'll have to plan it, and keep it hidden from him,' said Halina anxiously.

But when she got home and closed the front door, she felt defeated and forgot about her escape plans. She started making dinner, hoping Sean would be in a good mood this night — but he wasn't. They sat eating their dinner in silence, then he started.

'Why are you always wearing that ugly necklace?

It looks like something a witch would wear. You're a Catholic, I don't like it … take it off,' said Sean.

'No. It belongs in my family, why does it bother you?'

'I told you it's ugly, like our lie of a marriage. Take it off or I'll rip it off,' said Sean, pushing his chair back and standing up.

Halina jumped up and moved away, watching his movements. She had to guess right to avoid him grabbing her. Christine's words echoed in her mind and it dawned on her that time may be running out — she had to leave Sean to save herself. She was so fed up with this life and living in fear, but she wasn't going to take a beating easily this night; she was going to fight back. Sean had threatened to kill her so many times, but she never really believed he would do such a thing — she thought he was just trying to scare her.

He started with the usual verbal abuse.

'I'll never be a father with you as a wife; you and all your education and money, you always thought you were better than me. There's only one way to rid myself of you and I should have done it long ago,' Sean spat the words at her.

He went to the cutlery drawer and pulled out a large knife. Halina froze with fear; all her courage disappeared and she suddenly felt so tired. He started yelling abuse again, intimidating her, breaking her will. 'Give me that necklace; I'll sell it, we could use the money. All those stupid stories about its powers, it's pagan nonsense. I'll bet Father McGregor would agree with me. I've spoken to him about us, he said it's our duty to have children … you are a witch.' His face was flushed and he sounded as if he was going insane.

'How dare you speak to him behind my back! It could be your fault we can't have children. You're not having the necklace … ever! It doesn't belong to you,' shouted back Halina defiantly. She clutched the necklace, protecting it — her black raven, so beautiful, so warm to touch. She would never give it up. He would have to kill her first.

She ran down the hall to her room and grabbed the sewing scissors she had left on her dresser;

her heart was beating so fast now. She heard him coming and prepared to defend herself against his violence.

His eyes never left her face; he enjoyed watching the terror he saw there. His teeth were bared like a hungry animal. The first blow split her brow; she felt the wetness running down her face, the blood blinding her vision. Halina wiped it away quickly, keeping her attention on her husband's movements. She managed to dodge the next blow aimed at her nose; it glanced off, catching the side of her ear and making it numb. He pushed her against the wall, angry that he had missed; Halina clutched the scissors but just couldn't use them. Halina could tell he was in a terrible rage and was losing control — and he still had the knife.

It seemed unreal at first, like in slow motion; she saw the thrusting movement of his arm, then felt the firm thud against her chest. It felt like she had been punched hard and winded, then the pain changed to a sharp intensity and the blood spurted out. Halina knew she would die this night. He withdrew the knife and stabbed her again, lower down; the pain was awful and a weakness started to spread through her body and down her legs. Then he stabbed her again, this time into her shoulder; Halina screamed in agony, clutching at her wounds. The necklace chain snapped as it swung out of her torn clothing, covered in blood; it now shined red instead of black.

Halina saw the black raven, its eye staring as she crumpled to the ground. Something rose in her; an energy filled her body, as all her weakness left her.

Her husband leant forward, eager to finish his wife's life for good. That's when she squeezed the scissors and plunged them into her husband's neck, cutting his jugular vein. His expression changed to shock, and then he felt the pain and horror when he saw his blood pumping out like a fountain from the gaping wound. He straightened, stepped back then collapsed, clutching at his neck, gasping for breath; his blood formed a thick red pool around him as it poured out through his fingers. His legs jerked a couple of times then he laid still, his open eyes staring up at his dying wife.

Halina felt her life ebbing away, all her energy gone and her body now cold. It was difficult to focus and stay upright; her legs finally buckled under her and she fell to the floor, finally leaving her painful world behind. The black raven came to life, calling loudly, announcing its presence to Halina's soul, its oily feathers spread into huge wings and the power of the Morrigan was released. It freed Halina's soul from its body of flesh and suffering – and merged it with another, who had waited for a long time to be reunited with her true love. The Goddess deemed these souls worthy of such a gift, and now the promise had been fulfilled.

The ship rose and fell with the waves. The carved lady stood on the prow of *The Sea Witch*, boldly facing the waves. The salty breeze filled the sails and blew Sofia's long hair free; she turned and looked up into her lover's face. He was just as she remembered him, his dark eyes and curly hair, always so calm and observant … her brave pirate.

He looked into her eyes and smiled; she was just as beautiful as he remembered. Then he lifted the necklace, holding it in his palm, feeling the warmth of the stone before letting it fall against her dress.

'I knew the necklace would return you to me, my love.'

Pagan gods are mortal and immortal; their life is a perennial drama, which ever begins and ends, and is ever being renewed — a reflection of the life of nature itself.

(MacCulloch, 1918)

Bibliography

Daimler, Morgan (2014), *Pagan Portals – The Morrigan: Meeting the Great Queens*, page 9

Macalister, R. (1941), *Lebor Gabala Erenn, Volume IV*, page 20

MacCulloch, J. (1918), *Celtic Mythology*, page 33

Wikipedia, 'Magdalene Laundries in Ireland', (https://en.wikipedia.org/wiki/ Magdalene_Laundries_in_Ireland)

Polish and Russian names sources: www.baby-nameguide.com, www.babyname wizard.com.

Map of Poland: www.worldatlas.com, www.babble.com.

Also by the Author

Lisa, an Australian girl on holidays with her parents in Chile, makes friends with a local girl named Ximena who is no ordinary girl — her best friends are dolphins!

Together, the two girls form an incredible bond with the sea and the dolphins while facing great dangers. Dive into the water and share a fantastic adventure with these magical creatures.

Set amongst the beautiful scenery of Chile, ancient home of the Incas, this is a story of friendship, courage, love and the magic of life.

Beautiful! Silver Souls by Susan Vinson is a charming story, mystical, yet powerful too. Lovers of travel, legends and fables will be entranced by this tale.
—Alison Lewis, author *Seasons of Life & Missing*